A ROBIN
INVITED ME TO DINNER
L. D. ZINGG

Published by L.D. Zingg, LLC

Cover design and illustrations by Bonnie Lou Coleman

Edited by Jennifer Zingg

Format by John Ingle

ISBN-13: 978-1794203662

First Edition: 2019.01

LDZingg@gmail.com

FaceBook: LD Zingg

Available at Amazon.com

Dedication

To the innocent trust and adventurous spirit in every child.

Acknowledgments

A special thanks to my family and friends
for their encouragement and critiques.

A special thanks to my daughter, Jennifer,
for her direction and edits,
and to John Ingle, without whose assistance,
the publication of this book would not have been possible.

Other books by this author

THE POETRY OF LIFE

Novel Series

DESTINY OF A COP

LIARS ALL

THE LIGHT OF TRUTH

WHERE IT ALL BEGAN

Children's books

Barnyard Friends

I met a friendly Robin
On my Sunday morning stroll.
I'd planned to walk at least a mile
And had nearly reached my goal.

"Good morning, Mr. Robin,"
I said as I passed him by.
I thought that he would hop away
Or maybe even fly.

"Good morning, back to you my friend,"
The Robin boldly said.
"You probably think you're dreaming
Even though you aren't in bed.

I finally gathered all my wits
And stopped to think things through.
Was my imagination taking hold,
Or was it really true?

I've not gone daft, I told myself,
It was clear as clear could be.
I calmed myself and accepted the fact
That a bird had talked to me.

The Robin cocked a wary eye and said,
"You're looking pale.
I see you every morning
Walking fast along the trail.

Since I am always cautious
With strange creatures and with bears,
I started to decline his bid,
But manners softened fears.

"There won't be many there," he said
As he saw my hesitation.
"Just relatives and friends I know
Who've flown across the nation."

So I agreed to join the fest,
But asked where it would be.
"A barn is always best," he said.
"Either there or in a tree."

Well, I'm not much on climbing trees.
High places scare me silly.
I tend to buckle at the knees
When I think of something hilly.

So we gathered around some bales of hay
That were set up like a table.
I hadn't eaten quite that way
Since I was grown and able.

I wondered what the food would be
As each one brought a dish.
Maybe something from the surging sea-
A lobster or a fish.

I was dressed up in my finest.
He was in his finest too.
The red vest he was wearing
Looked well fitted and brand new.

He was pleased that I agreed to dine
With him and all his cousins.
There were doves and pigeons, oh so fine,
And sparrows by the dozens.

When everyone was gathered 'round,
The turtle dove said Grace.
And goodwill did indeed abound
And flourish in this place.

I'd worked up quite an appetite
And was hungry as could be.
For I hadn't eaten a single bite
Since the dawn had awakened me.

When the food was served I realized
The folly I had made.
But I didn't want to be impolite
Or act as if afraid.

I nibbled some, but couldn't choke down
Even a morsel more.
As I saw the bulging bowls
That he'd brought up from his store.

So children if you're asked to dine
With a strange but friendly Robin,
And even if he smiles a lot
And his head just keeps on bobbin'.

Tell him you have other plans
And make your answer firm.
For the items on his menu are:

Beastly Beetles...Creepy Crickets...
Grimy Grasshoppers...Slimy Snails...
And a Big...Fat...Worm.